HEINEMANN GUID
ELEMENTARY

C000024817

JOHN STEINBECK
The Red Pony

Retold by M.J. Paine

HEINEMANN

ELEMENTARY LEVEL

Series Editor: John Milne

The Heinemann Guided Readers provide a choice of enjoyable reading material for learners of English. The series is published at five levels – Starter, Beginner, Elementary, Intermediate and Upper. At **Elementary Level**, the control of content and language has the following main features:

Information Control

Stories have straightforward plots and a restricted number of main characters. Information which is vital to the understanding of the story is clearly presented and repeated when necessary. Difficult allusion and metaphor are avoided and cultural backgrounds are made explicit.

Structure Control

Students will meet those grammatical features which they have already been taught in their elementary course of studies. Other grammatical features occasionally occur with which the students may not be so familiar, but their use is made clear through context and reinforcement. This ensures that the reading as well as being enjoyable provides a continual learning situation for the students. Sentences are kept short – a maximum of two clauses in nearly all cases – and within sentences there is a balanced use of simple adverbial and adjectival phrases. Great care is taken with pronoun reference.

Vocabulary Control

At **Elementary Level** there is a limited use of a carefully controlled vocabulary of approximately 1,100 basic words. At the same time, students are given some opportunity to meet new or unfamiliar words in contexts where their meaning is obvious. The meaning of words introduced in this way is reinforced by repetition. Help is also given to the students in the form of vivid illustrations which are closely related to the text.

Contents

The People in This Story

Jody Tiflin

Billy Buck

Carl Tiflin

Mrs Tiflin

THE GIFT

1

A Visit To Salinas

Billy Buck was always the first person to get up. He went to
the barn and opened the door. Then he picked up the brush
and started to brush the first horse. Billy had just finished
the second horse when he heard the triangle.

Mrs Tiflin stood on the porch and rang the triangle
loudly. Billy put down the brush and went over to the
porch. He sat on the steps and waited. Billy never started
his breakfast before the family.

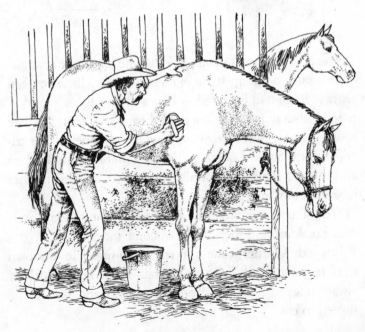

The boy, Jody, was sleeping. When he heard the triangle, he woke up and jumped out of bed. Jody was a little boy, ten years old. He had light yellow hair and grey eyes.

Jody always jumped when he heard the triangle. The sound was an order to get up. Everybody obeyed the triangle. Jody dressed quickly. Then he went to the kitchen and washed himself. He finished washing and his mother looked at him angrily.

'Your hair is too long,' she said. 'I must cut it today. Start your breakfast and then Billy can come in.'

But Jody's father came into the room first. He sat down next to Jody. Carl Tiflin was a tall, stern man and Jody always obeyed him. Carl took some eggs and bacon and started to eat.

Billy Buck heard the family having breakfast. He stood up and went into the house. He took some eggs from the plate and sat down.

'Have you got the cows ready to go to Salinas, Billy?' Carl Tiflin asked. 'We must get to town early.'

'Yes, they're ready,' answered Billy. 'I can easily take them to town alone.'

'Of course you can,' said Carl laughing. 'But I want to come with you. Perhaps we can have a drink together.'

'What time will you get back, Carl?' Mrs Tiflin asked.

'I don't know,' Carl answered. 'I've got to see some men in Salinas. Perhaps we won't get back until it's dark.'

After breakfast, Jody followed his father and Billy Buck out of the house. Then the two men rode over the hill towards Salinas. They were going to sell some cows in the market.

When Carl and Billy had gone, Jody walked back to the house. His mother gave him his books and his lunch bag. On his way to school, Jody filled his pockets with stones. Every now and again, he threw a stone at a bird or a rabbit. Near the bridge, Jody met two friends. The three boys walked happily to school, laughing and joking together.

Jody arrived home at four o'clock. Jody's father was not back from the town. Jody's mother was sitting outside the house.

'There are some cakes for you in the kitchen.' she said.

Jody went to the kitchen and came back eating a cake.

'Make sure you fill up the wood box,' his mother said. 'It was only half-full last night. And look more carefully in the grass for the hens' eggs.'

Jody filled the wood box and then went into the woods with his rifle. He pointed the rifle at rocks and birds and trees, but he did not shoot. He had no cartridges in his gun. His father was going to give him cartridges when Jody was twelve years old.

2

A Pony For Jody

Carl Tiflin and Billy Buck came back in the evening and they all had supper. After supper, Jody sat by the fireplace and listened to his father. Jody wanted to hear the news from the town. Then his father looked at him.

'Go to bed, Jody,' Carl Tiflin said, 'I'm going to need you in the morning.'

'What are we going to do in the morning?' Jody asked.

'You'll find out tomorrow,' his father answered. 'Now, go to bed!'

The triangle woke Jody up in the morning and he dressed quickly. He went to the kitchen and washed his face.

'Don't go out until you've eaten a good breakfast,' said his mother.

Jody sat down at the long, white table. Then Jody's father and Billy Buck came in. Carl Tiflin looked stern, and Billy did not look at Jody at all.

'You come with us after breakfast,' Carl Tiflin said to Jody.

The men finished their coffee, stood up and went outside. Jody followed them a little way behind.

'Carl,' Mrs Tiflin suddenly called, 'don't keep Jody too long. He must go to school.'

They walked through the field to the barn. Jody's father opened the door and they went in. The barn was dark inside and Jody could not see very well.

'Come here,' Carl Tiflin ordered.

Jody began to see things more clearly. He looked into a stall and stepped back quickly. A red pony was looking at

Jody out of the stall. The pony's ears were forward and its eyes were shining. Jody was so excited that he could not speak.

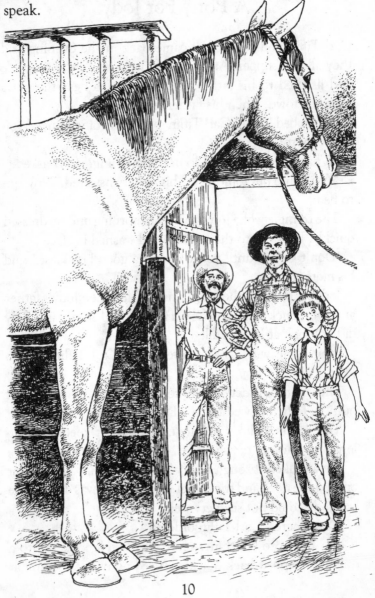

3

'Gabilan'

Jody looked at the pony.

'Mine?' he asked.

No one answered. Then Carl Tiflin spoke.

'The pony needs a good brushing,' he said. 'And don't forget to feed it. And don't leave the stall dirty. If you don't look after the pony, I'll sell it straight away.'

Jody put his hand out to the pony. The animal's grey nose came close and sniffed loudly. Then the pony gently bit Jody's fingers and shook its head up and down.

Jody looked at his fingers.

'Well,' he said, 'the pony can certainly bite!'

The two men laughed. Then Carl Tiflin went out of the barn, but Billy Buck stayed.

'Is the pony mine?' Jody asked again.

'Yes,' Billy answered. 'But you must look after the pony and train him. I'll show you how to train him. He's only a colt. He's still very young, so you can't ride him for some time.'

Jody put out his hand again. This time the boy rubbed the pony's nose.

'He wants a carrot,' Jody said. 'Where did you get him, Billy?'

'We bought the pony at the market.'

'Is there a saddle?' asked Jody.

'Oh, yes, I'd forgotten. Here it is.'

Billy took down a little saddle from the wall. The saddle was made of shining red leather.

'This saddle isn't very strong,' he said. 'But it was cheap.'

Jody rubbed the red saddle with his fingers.

'It'll look very pretty on the pony,' he said.

Then Jody thought for a moment.

'Has the pony got a name yet?' he asked.

'Not yet,' said Billy.

'Then I'll call him Gabilan Mountains.'

'That name's too long,' Billy said. 'Why don't you call him Gabilan? That is a fine name for him.'

'Can I take Gabilan to school with me?' Jody asked. 'I want to show him to my friends.'

But Billy shook his head.

'The pony isn't trained yet,' he said. 'Your father and I had to pull him here. But you must go to school now.'

'I'll bring my friends here this afternoon,' Jody said. 'Then they can see Gabilan.'

4

Boys From School

That afternoon, six boys came running over the hill. They went into the barn and looked at the pony. Then they looked at Jody. Jody had a pony now and so he was different. The boys watched and Gabilan put his nose out of the stall and sniffed.

'Why don't you ride him?' the boys asked. 'When are you going to ride him?'

'He's not old enough. Nobody can ride him for a long time. Billy Buck is going to show me how to train him.'

'Well, can we take the pony out into the corral?'

'No, we can't,' replied Jody.

Jody wanted to be alone when he took the pony out for the first time.

'Come and see the saddle,' he said.

The boys looked at the saddle with wide open eyes.

'The saddle isn't very strong, but it'll look pretty on Gabilan,' Jody said.

The boys went home and Jody took a brush and comb from the wall. Then he went into the stall. The pony's eyes shone and Jody touched Gabilan on the shoulder. Then Jody rubbed the pony's neck.

'Quiet, boy. Sh!' Jody whispered in a deep voice.

The pony stood still and Jody brushed and combed him.

Jody did not hear his mother come into the barn. She was angry at first. Then she saw Jody working and she felt very proud.

'Have you forgotten the wood box?' she asked gently. 'It's nearly dark and there's no wood in the house. And you must feed the chickens, too.'

'I forgot, ma'am,' Jody said.

'Well, do your work before you brush the pony. Then you won't forget.'

'Can I have carrots from the garden for Gabilan?' Jody asked.

'Yes, of course. But take the big, old ones.'

'Carrots are good for a pony,' said Jody.

And again, Jody's mother felt proud of her son.

5

The Rain Starts

Jody never waited for the triangle now. He woke up and jumped out of bed before his mother was up. Then he ran down to the barn. He opened the door very quietly, but Gabilan was always looking at Jody out of the stall. The pony stamped his foot when he saw the boy.

Sometimes Billy Buck was in the barn. He was getting the work horses ready. Then Jody and Billy stood and looked at Gabilan together. Billy told Jody a lot of things about horses. Billy's own horse was an Indian pony and he always won first prize at competitions. Billy knew all about horses, so Jody always listened carefully.

Billy Buck and Jody started training Gabilan in the early autumn. Every morning, they took the pony into the corral. They taught Gabilan to gallop round at the end of a long rope. One day, Jody's father came and watched.

'We must soon put the saddle on Gabilan,' Carl Tiflin said.

They taught Gabilan to gallop round at the end of a long rope.

Jody ran to the barn and came back with the saddle. At first, Gabilan did not like the saddle on his back. But, after a few days, Gabilan was happy with the saddle.

Then they had to put the bit in the pony's mouth. At first, Gabilan tried to rub the straps off his head. Sometimes the pony rubbed very hard and a little blood came from his mouth. But at last, Gabilan was happy with the bit, too.

'You can ride him soon,' Carl Tiflin said one day.

Time went slowly. Winter was coming. Clouds began to fill the sky. The wind blew hard at night. Jody did not want it to rain, but the rain came. It rained for a whole week. Gabilan stayed in the stable all the time. Then one day, the sun came out brightly.

'I'll leave Gabilan in the corral when I go to school today,' Jody said to Billy Buck.

'The sun will do him good,' Billy answered. 'Animals don't like being inside too long. Your father and I are going up the hill. We've got some work to do up there.'

'But, perhaps it will rain . . .' said Jody.

'It won't rain today.'

And so Jody went to school and Gabilan stayed outside in the corral.

6

Billy Buck's Mistake

Billy Buck was not wrong about many things. But he was wrong about the rain that day. A little after midday, the clouds turned black and the rain began to fall heavily. Jody heard the rain on the school roof. When school finished, he ran home through the rain.

Jody saw Gabilan from the top of the hill. The pony was standing in the corral. His coat was heavy with rain and his head was hanging low.

Jody ran down the hill. He opened the barn door and led the pony inside. Then he rubbed Gabilan all over with a sack. The pony stood quietly, but his legs were shaking all the time.

Jody dried Gabilan and brought some hot water. Jody mixed the water with some grain, but Gabilan was not very hungry. The pony tried to eat, but he didn't want the food. Gabilan stood there with his legs shaking.

Billy Buck and Carl Tiflin came back in the evening.

*Then he rubbed Gabilan all over with a sack. The pony stood
quietly, but his legs were shaking all the time.*

'The rain didn't stop all the afternoon,' Carl Tiflin said. 'We stayed at Ben's house on the hill.'

Jody looked at Billy Buck and Billy quickly looked the other way.

'You said it wasn't going to rain!' Jody said. 'The pony got wet!'

'Did you dry him?' asked Billy.

'I rubbed him with a sack and I gave him some hot grain.'

Billy nodded his head.

'Will Gabilan be all right, Billy?' asked Jody.

'A little rain never hurt anybody,' Billy replied. 'Did you put a blanket over his back?'

'No, I couldn't find a blanket,' Jody answered. 'I put some sacks over him.'

'We'll cover Gabilan up after supper,' Billy said.

Jody felt better then. After supper, Billy and Jody walked through the mud to the barn. The barn was dark and warm.

Billy felt Gabilan's legs. He put his face against the pony's head. Then he looked into Gabilan's eyes and mouth.

'He doesn't look very well,' Billy said. 'I'll give him a good rub.'

Then Billy found a sack and rubbed the pony's legs and chest. But Gabilan stood still without moving. Billy brought a heavy blanket and put it over the pony's back. He tied the blanket round Gabilan with string.

'He'll be all right in the morning,' Billy said.

When Jody got back to the house, his mother looked at him.

'You're late for bed,' she said.

She held Jody and brushed the hair out of his eyes.

'Don't worry about the pony,' she said. 'He'll be all right. Billy's a good horse doctor.'

19

But Jody worried about Gabilan all night. He heard the clock strike two o'clock and then he fell asleep. When he woke up, it was daylight outside. Jody jumped out of bed, put on his clothes and ran to the barn. In the barn, Billy was rubbing the pony's legs. Billy looked up and smiled.

'He's got a little cold,' Billy said. 'He'll be outside in the corral in a few days.'

Jody looked at the pony's face. Gabilan's eyes were half closed. The corners of his eyes were wet. The pony's ears hung down and his head was bent low. Jody put out his hand, but the pony did not move.

'He's very sick, Billy,' Jody said.

'Only a little cold,' Billy answered. 'You have some breakfast and then go to school. I'll take care of Gabilan. Tomorrow's Saturday. You can stay with him all day.'

7

Gabilan Is Sick

At school that day, Jody could not answer any questions. He could not read any words. He did not tell anyone that the pony was sick.

School finished and Jody walked slowly home. He did not want to go home and see Gabilan.

Billy was in the barn, but Gabilan was worse. The pony's eyes were almost closed and he could not breathe through his nose.

'Is Gabilan going to be all right, Billy?' Jody asked.

Billy put his fingers under the pony's neck.

'Feel here,' Billy said.

Jody put his hand on the pony's neck and felt a large lump. Then Billy spoke again.

'When that lump gets bigger, I'll open it. Then Gabilan will get better.'

'What's wrong with him?' Jody asked.

Billy did not want to answer, but he had to.

'Oh, don't worry about him,' he said. 'I'll make him well. I'm going to give him some steam now. You can help.'

Billy put some medicine in a nosebag. He put the nosebag over the pony's head. Then Billy poured some water through a hole in the side of the bag. Gabilan jumped back at first. Then the steam went up his nose and he began to breathe more easily. When Billy took the nosebag off, the pony breathed and his eyes opened a little wider.

'He feels a little better now,' Billy said. 'Now we'll put the blanket over him again. Perhaps he'll be well by the morning.'

'I'll stay with him tonight,' Jody said.

'No, don't you do that,' Billy said. 'I'll bring some blankets and sleep here. You can stay tomorrow and give Gabilan some steam.'

That evening, Mrs Tiflin filled the wood box, but Jody did not notice. And, at supper, his father told stories, but Jody was not listening.

'Isn't that a funny story?' Carl Tiflin asked.

'Yes, sir,' Jody answered, but he did not laugh.

Jody's father was angry then and he did not tell any more stories.

After a while, Jody went down to the barn. Billy Buck was asleep in the hay. Gabilan was breathing loudly, but he looked much better. Jody rubbed his fingers over the pony's red coat. Then Jody went back to the house. When he was in bed, his mother came into the room.

'The pony will be all right,' she said.

Jody was tired and went to sleep quickly. He awoke early in the morning when the triangle rang. He met Billy in the kitchen.

'How is Gabilan?' Jody asked.

'He's all right,' Billy answered. 'I'm going to open the lump this morning. Then perhaps he'll be much better.'

After breakfast, Billy took out his best knife. He sharpened the knife on a stone.

Jody looked at Gabilan in the barn. He knew immediately that the pony was worse. Gabilan's eyes were shut tight. His head hung low and he was breathing loudly.

Billy lifted the pony's head. Then he quickly cut the

22

lump. Jody held Gabilan's head and Billy washed the cut.

'Now he'll feel better.' Billy said.

Jody looked at Billy, but he did not believe him.

'He's very sick,' Jody said.

Billy thought for a long time.

'Yes, he's very sick,' he said. 'But I've seen sick ponies before and they've got better. He'll be all right, Jody. You stay with him. If Gabilan gets worse, you can come and get me.'

Billy went away and Jody stood beside the pony. Jody rubbed Gabilan behind the ears, but the pony did not move. Gabilan breathed louder and louder.

Later in the morning, Billy Buck came back and made another steam bag. Billy put the bag on Gabilan's head and Jody watched. The pony breathed a little better, but his head still hung low.

Saturday went very slowly. In the evening, Jody went to the house and brought back some blankets. That night, he slept in the barn and kept a lantern burning. Every now and again, Jody got up and rubbed Gabilan's legs.

At nine o'clock the wind started to blow strongly round the barn. But Jody was very tired and he fell asleep. Then, in the middle of the night, he heard a loud noise. Jody jumped up and looked around. The barn door was open and Gabilan was gone.

Billy Tries To Help

Jody quickly took the lantern and ran outside into the wind. Gabilan was running away into the darkness. Jody ran after the pony and caught him. Then he led Gabilan back to the stall. When Gabilan was in the stall again, the pony's breathing grew louder and louder.

Jody was glad when Billy Buck came into the barn. Billy looked at Gabilan for a long time. Then he felt the pony's legs.

'Jody,' Billy said, 'I want to do something. I don't want you to look. Run into the house for a while.'

'You're not going to shoot him, are you?' asked Jody.

'No,' replied Billy. 'His nose is filled up. He can't breathe easily. I'm going to cut a little hole in his neck. He'll be able to breathe then.'

'I'll stay here,' said Jody.

'All right,' Billy told Jody. 'You can hold his head. But don't look if it makes you feel sick.'

Billy sharpened his knife again. Jody held Gabilan's head and Billy felt for the right place. The knife went into Gabilan's neck and tears ran down Jody's cheeks. The pony jumped back and then stood there shaking. Blood ran out over the knife and onto Billy's hand and shirt. Billy's strong hand cut out a round hole in the pony's neck. Gabilan began to breathe again through the hole.

Billy did a good job. He cleaned the wound and the blood stopped. Gabilan breathed easily.

The triangle rang and Jody walked slowly out of the barn. After breakfast, Jody's mother gave him some hot grain for the pony.

'Give Gabilan this,' she said.

'He won't eat anything,' Jody answered.

Then Jody ran back to the barn without the hot grain. In the barn, Billy Buck showed Jody how to keep the wound clean.

Carl Tiflin came into the barn too. He looked at the pony. Then he turned to his son.

'Come with me, Jody,' he said. 'I'm going to drive over the hill.'

Jody shook his head.

'Come away from the barn,' Carl Tiflin said.

Then Billy Buck turned angrily.

'Leave Jody alone,' he said. 'Gabilan is Jody's horse, isn't he?'

Carl Tiflin did not say another word. He walked out of the barn.

9

A Place To Die

At midday, the pony lay down on his side. The pony's hair looked dry and dead. Jody had seen dead hair on a dog. He knew now that Gabilan was dying.

Jody watched Gabilan all the afternoon. Just before dark Mrs Tiflin brought Jody some food. He ate a little of it. He hung up the lantern near Gabilan's head. Then the boy wrapped himself in his blanket and fell asleep. In the night, the wind blew again and the farm doors banged.

When Jody woke up, it was daylight. Gabilan had gone again. Jody jumped up and ran out into the morning light.

Jody found the pony's tracks in the grass. The tracks led towards the woods. Jody started to run. He saw a dark shadow on the ground. Jody looked up and saw some black buzzards. The big birds flew lower and lower and went down behind a hill. Jody ran faster and faster.

Jody looked down and saw Gabilan. The red pony was lying under a tree. The buzzards stood round the pony. The big birds were waiting for the pony's death.

Jody ran down the hill. When he reached Gabilan, a large buzzard was sitting on the pony's head. The other birds flew away. But the buzzard on Gabilan's head did not move.

Jody caught the bird's wing and pulled it to the ground. The buzzard was nearly as big as Jody. The bird's wings beat into Jody's face. Its sharp claws gripped the boy's legs. Jody held the buzzard by the neck and did not let go.

Jody held the buzzard on the ground with his knee. He picked up a big stone and beat the bird's head. He beat the bird's head again and again until the bird was dead. Jody was still beating the dead bird when Billy Buck pulled him away.

The bird's wings beat into Jody's face

*Jody was still beating the dead bird when Billy Buck
pulled him away*

Carl Tiflin wiped the blood from Jody's face with a handkerchief. Then he kicked the buzzard away with his boot.

'Jody,' he said, 'the buzzard didn't kill the pony. Don't you know that?'

'I know,' said Jody. 'I know.'

But Billy Buck was angry. He lifted Jody into his arms and started to carry the boy home. Then he looked at Carl Tiflin.

'Of course he knows that!' Billy said angrily. 'Can't you see how Jody feels!'

THE GREAT MOUNTAINS

1

Old Gitano

It was the middle of summer and Jody had nothing to do. He was bored. The boy lay on his back in the grass. He was looking at the mountains in the distance. Jody had never been to the mountains.

'What's on the other side?' he asked his father.

'More mountains,' Carl Tiflin answered.

'More and more mountains?' asked Jody.

'Well, no,' said his father. 'In the end you come to the sea.'

'But what's in the mountains?'

'A few people. But it's a dangerous place with great big rocks and things. There's not much water. Only some rocks and trees. Why?'

'I'd like to go there,' said Jody.

'What for?' his father asked. 'There's nothing there.'

Then Jody went to the kitchen.

'Do you know what's in the mountains?' he asked his mother.

'Only the bears,' she said.

'What bears?' asked Jody.

His mother did not reply.

Then Jody asked Billy Buck about the mountains.

'There's nothing in the mountains,' Billy said. 'There's nothing to eat. There's only rocks and people can't eat rocks!'

Jody never learned any more about the mountains. And

all that summer he thought about the secret places in the high mountains.

One day, Jody saw a man walking over the hill from Salinas. The man was coming towards the house. The man was thin and straight and very old. He walked slowly and stiffly. The old man was dressed in blue jeans and an old coat. He wore big boots and an old hat. The man carried a sack over his shoulder.

The old man came closer. His skin was brown and he had a white moustache. The old man's eyes were large and dark.

The old man came close to the gate and put down his sack.

'Do you live here?' he said to Jody.

Jody turned and looked back to the barn. Nobody was there. Then Jody turned and looked at the old man again.

'Yes,' Jody answered.

'I have come back,' the old man said. 'I am Gitano, and I have come back.'

Jody did not know what to say. He turned and ran to the house. Jody's mother was in the kitchen.

'An old man is here,' Jody said. 'And he says that he's come back.'

'Well, what does he want?' Jody's mother asked.

'I don't know,' said Jody. 'The old man came here from over the hill.'

One day, Jody saw a man walking over the hill from Salinas.
The man was thin and straight and very old.

Gitano stood up and put on his hat.

An old horse was in the corral.

'That's old Easter,' Jody said. 'Easter is thirty years old.'

'He's no good any more,' Gitano said. 'Too old to work.
He eats up food – that's all. Soon he'll die.'

Carl Tiflin heard Gitano's words.

'I must shoot old Easter,' Carl Tiflin said. 'It's kinder to
shoot old things. One shot, a big noise and the horse is dead.'

Then Billy Buck spoke.

'Easter has worked hard all his life. He needs a rest now.'

'It's better to shoot old horses,' Carl Tiflin said.

'Let him rest,' Billy answered.

Then Carl and Billy went back to the house.

'My father's only talking,' Jody said. 'He won't shoot
Easter. He likes Easter. That was my father's first horse.'

'But Easter's no good any more,' Gitano answered.

That evening, Jody saw a light in Gitano's room. The old
man was sitting back in a chair. Jody pushed the door open
and went in. Gitano sat up quickly. He was holding a
beautiful golden sword in his hand.

'What is it?' Jody asked. 'Can I see it?'

The old man put the sword under the lamp.

'Where did you get it from?' Jody asked.

'I got it from my father,' replied Gitano.

'Where did he get the sword?' asked the boy.

'I don't know,' said Gitano.

'What do you do with it?'

'Nothing,' replied the old man.

Then Gitano wrapped the sword in a cloth.

'You must go now,' he said. 'I want to go to bed.'

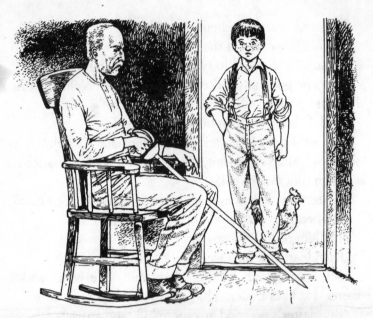

Jody walked back to the house. He thought about the old man's secret. Jody did not tell anyone about the sword.

The next morning, Jody was first at the breakfast table.

Then Jody's father came in. Billy Buck came in last. Mrs Tiflin looked in from the kitchen.

'Where's the old man?' she asked.

'Maybe he's already gone,' Carl Tiflin said.

4

An Old Man And An Old Horse

After breakfast Jody looked in Gitano's room. The old man was not there. Then Jody went back to the house. His father was outside the kitchen.

'I think that old Easter is dead at last,' he said. 'He didn't come out of the barn with the other horses.'

Then a man from another farm rode by.

'Did you sell your old horse, Carl?' the man asked.

'No, of course not,' Carl answered. 'Why?'

'Well, early this morning, I saw an old man on an old horse. The horse had no saddle. The old man was riding across the fields. He was holding something. I think it was a gun.'

'That's old Gitano,' Carl Tiflin said. 'Perhaps he's taken one of my guns.'

Carl went into the house for a moment. Then he came back.

'No,' he said. 'All my guns are there. Which way was he going?'

'Well, it's very strange,' the man said. 'He was going towards the mountains.'

Then Carl Tiflin laughed.

'Men are never too old to steal,' he said. 'He's stolen old Easter.'

'Do you want to go after him?' the man asked.

'No,' replied Carl Tiflin. 'That old horse is ready to die. But what does Gitano want in the mountains?'

Jody walked to the back of the house. He looked towards the mountains. Jody thought of the sword and of old Gitano. Jody thought of the great lonely mountains. He lay down in the green grass. He covered his eyes with his arms and lay there for a long time. And Jody felt very lonely and sad.

THE PROMISE

1

A Colt For Nellie

It was spring. Jody was coming back from school. The hills were covered with green grass. The trees on the hills were green, too.

Suddenly, Jody stopped walking. He bent down on his knees. He picked up a toad by the side of the road. The little animal tried to escape, but Jody held it. Then Jody opened his lunch box and put the toad inside. Jody walked towards home. Before he reached the farm, he caught two more toads and some other small animals. He put them all in his lunch box.

Jody opened the kitchen door and his mother looked up from her work.

'Oh, Jody,' she said. 'Your father wants to see you.'

'What for? Did I do something wrong?'

Jody's mother laughed.

'What did you do?' she asked.

'Nothing!' Jody replied.

'That's all right, then,' said Mrs Tiflin. 'But your father wants to see you. He's down by the barn.'

Jody went out of the back door. His mother opened his lunch box and cried out, angrily. Then Jody ran off towards the barn. His mother called from the back door, but Jody had gone.

Carl Tiflin and Billy Buck were standing against a fence. They were watching some horses in the field. They were looking at the mare, Nellie. She was standing against the gate.

Jody walked up to his father and Billy Buck. The boy stood quietly beside the men. The two men looked at him.

'I wanted to see you,' said Carl Tiflin.

'Yes, sir.'

'Billy says that you took good care of Gabilan before the pony died.'

'Yes, sir. I did,' Jody said.

'Billy says you are good with horses,' said his father.

Jody did not answer, but he smiled at Billy Buck.

'Jody trained that pony well,' Billy said.

'If I get you another horse, will you work hard?' Carl asked.

Jody's eyes opened wide with excitement.

'Yes, sir.'

'Well then, I want Nellie to have a colt,' said his father. 'It's time she was a mother again.'

'Nellie's going to be a mother?' the boy said excitedly.

Then Carl Tiflin spoke again.

'Jess Taylor lives at the farm on the hill. He's got a good stallion. It'll be the father of Nellie's colt. You'll have to take care of Nellie until she has her colt. Will you do that?'

'Yes, sir,' replied Jody immediately.

'Well, all right then,' his father said. 'Tomorrow you can take Nellie up to Jess Taylor's stallion.'

'Yes, sir.'

'Now go and feed the chickens and get the wood.'

2

Jess Taylor's Stallion

Jody worked hard. He fed the chickens and filled up the wood box to the top. Then he went to his mother.

'I'm sorry about the toads in my lunch box,' he said. 'I'll never do that again.'

Later that evening, Jody climbed to the top of the fence. He looked at Nellie. Billy Buck was carrying a bucket of milk towards the house. He saw Jody and stopped.

'It's a long time to wait,' Billy said gently. 'You'll get very tired of waiting.'

'No, I won't. But how long will it be, before Nellie has her colt?'

'Nearly a year,' replied Billy.

'I won't get tired of waiting,' said the boy.

The triangle rang for supper. Jody climbed down from the fence. Then he and Billy carried the bucket to the house.

The next morning after breakfast, Billy Buck put some reins on Nellie. Then he led her out of the field. Jody took the reins and started up the hill.

After about an hour, Jody turned into a narrow road. The road led to Jess Taylor's farm. Jody saw the red roof of the barn and he heard a dog barking.

Suddenly Nellie pulled her head up. A loud noise was coming from Jess Taylor's barn. The noise frightened Nellie and she jumped back. Then Jody heard a man's voice. Someone was shouting. Jody pulled the reins and Nellie tried to bite him. Jody dropped the reins and ran behind some trees.

Suddenly the stallion came down the hill. The horse was galloping fast and could not stop. Nellie's ears went back. She kicked the stallion as he went by. The stallion came back. He kicked Nellie with his front legs and bit the mare's neck. Then the two horses suddenly became quiet and stood beside each other. Jody watched from the trees.

Jess Taylor rode up quietly behind Jody. His big hand lifted the boy off the ground. Jess Taylor put Jody behind him on his horse.

'That stallion can kill you,' Jess said. 'He's dangerous sometimes. He broke his reins and went straight through the gate.'

'He'll hurt Nellie,' Jody cried. 'He'll kill her! Get him away!'

Jess Taylor laughed at the boy.

'Nellie will be all right,' Jess said. 'Why don't you jump down and go to the house for a while. My wife will give you a piece of pie.'

But Jody shook his head. He didn't want to leave Nellie.

'Nellie's mine, and the colt's going to be mine,' Jody said. 'I'm going to look after it.'

'Yes, that's a good thing,' said Jess. 'Your father has got some good sense sometimes.'

The danger passed and Jess Taylor lifted Jody down. Then Jess took the stallion's reins and rode ahead. Jody followed with Nellie.

In the farmhouse, Mrs Taylor gave Jody two pieces of pie. Then Jody left. Nellie followed quietly behind him. The mare was very quiet now. Jody climbed on her back and rode most of the way home.

The stallion came back. He kicked Nellie with his front legs.

3

Jody Waits

All that spring and summer, Jody worked hard. He felt that he had suddenly grown up. He helped cut the hay and looked after the horses. Carl Tiflin taught Jody to milk a cow. The boy had a lot of work to do now.

Jody went to see Nellie every day. He looked at the mare carefully, but he did not see any change. One day, Billy Buck walked up to Nellie and patted her neck.

'Is she really going to have a colt?' Jody asked.

Billy looked at Nellie's eyes and felt her stomach.

'I think so.'

'Three months have passed,' said Jody. 'She hasn't changed much.'

'Wait for another eight months,' Billy said. 'She'll have her colt then.'

'It's a long time, isn't it?' said the boy.

'And you won't be able to ride the colt for two more years,' said Billy.

'I'll be a man by then!'

Then Billy Buck laughed.

'You'll almost be an old man!' he said.

'What colour will the colt be?' Jody asked.

'I don't know,' said Billy. 'The stallion is black and Nellie is brown. The colt can be black or brown or grey. I don't know. Sometimes a black mare will have a white colt!'

'Well, I hope it's black. And I hope it's a stallion,' said Jody.

'Your father won't let you have a stallion. Stallions are too dangerous. They're always fighting and making trouble.'

'What happens when a mare has a colt?' Jody asked. 'Is it the same as cows with calves?'

'Yes, but a little more difficult. Sometimes you must help the mare. And sometimes there can be trouble . . .'

Billy stopped speaking.

'What kind of trouble?' Jody asked.

'Sometimes you must kill the colt or the mare will die,' replied Billy.

'It won't be like that with Nellie, will it?' asked Jody.

'Oh, no. Nellie has always had good colts before.'

'Can I be there?' the boy asked. 'Will you call me when it's time? You must call me because the colt is mine.'

'Yes,' said Billy. 'I'll call you. Of course I will.'

Jody and Billy turned and walked slowly down the hill towards the barn. Jody was worried.

'Billy, you won't let the colt die, will you?'

'Anything can happen,' Billy said. 'If something is wrong, it won't be my fault. I can't do everything. I'll do my best for Nellie. But I can't promise anything. Nellie is a good mare. She's had good colts before.'

Billy walked away from Jody. He did not say any more.

4

Another Three Months

The year passed slowly and Nellie did not change. The summer and the autumn passed. The wind began to blow and the air was colder.

It was a bright morning in September. Jody was finishing breakfast. His mother called him. She was pouring boiling water into a bucket full of corn.

'Watch how I do this,' she said, 'you'll have to do it soon.'

'What is it?' Jody asked.

'It's warm food for Nellie,' she said.

'Will Nellie ever have her colt?' Jody asked. 'Is she going to be all right?'

Mrs Tiflin put down the bucket.

'Of course Nellie will be all right,' she said. 'But you must take better care of her from now on. Here, take her breakfast out to her.'

Jody took the bucket and ran past the barn. He climbed the fence and put the bucket beside the mare. Jody stepped back and looked. Nellie had changed. The mare's stomach was bigger. She ate the food and pushed the bucket with her nose. Then she came over to Jody and rubbed her cheek against his arm.

Billy Buck came out of the barn.

'She's going to be all right,' he said.

Nellie put her head under Billy's arm and rubbed her neck up and down.

'You must take good care of Nellie, now,' Billy said.

'How long will it be?' asked Jody.

Billy counted on his fingers.

'About the middle of January. Another three months.'

'You will call me, won't you, Billy? You will let me be there, won't you?'

'Carl wants you to be there when the colt is born,' replied Billy. 'That's the way to learn. You have to see for yourself. That's the only way to learn about horses.'

'You know everything about horses, Billy, don't you?' said Jody.

Billy laughed at this.

'Yes,' he said. 'I'm nearly a horse myself. My mother died when I was born. My father was old and we lived in the mountains. We didn't have any cows and my father gave me mare's milk!'

Then Billy became serious. He looked at Nellie and spoke to her.

'And horses understand me. You understand me, don't you, Nellie?'

The mare turned her head and looked straight into Billy's eyes for a moment. And Billy felt proud of himself.

'I'll get you a good colt,' he said to Jody. 'You'll have the best horse in the country.'

And Jody felt very proud, too.

5

Jody Is Worried

Winter came quickly. When the rains began to fall, Jody put Nellie into a stall. He fed the mare with warm food every morning. Then Jody brushed and combed her.

The mare was getting very fat and Jody was worried.

One day, Billy put his hand against Nellie's stomach.

'Feel here,' Billy told Jody. 'Perhaps you can feel the colt move.'

Jody felt Nellie's stomach very carefully.

'I can't feel anything,' he said.

After that, Jody put his hand against Nellie's stomach twenty times a day. One day, he felt the colt moving. Nellie became more and more friendly. The mare rubbed her nose against Jody's arm.

Jody told his father about the colt and Carl Tiflin came into the barn. Carl looked at Nellie's coat and felt her stomach.

'You've done a very good job, Jody,' Carl Tiflin said.

Jody listened to these words and he felt very proud.

The fifteenth of January came and the colt was not born. Then the twentieth day came.

'Is she all right?' Jody asked.

'Of course,' Billy answered.

'Is she going to be all right?' Jody asked again.

Billy stroked the mare's neck.

'Every mare is different, Jody. You must wait.'

6

Jody Can't Sleep

When the end of the month arrived, Jody was very worried. Nellie was very big and she breathed heavily. One night, Jody could not sleep. He went quietly out to the barn. Jody found a lantern and a box of matches. He lit the lantern and walked towards Nellie's stall.

The mare was standing in her stall. Her whole body was moving from side to side. Jody put his hand on Nellie's shoulder and she shivered. Then Billy Buck looked up from his bed in the hay.

'Jody, what are you doing?' he said.

Jody looked at Billy lying in the hay.

'Do you think she's all right?' asked Jody.

'Of course she's all right,' Billy replied angrily. 'Now get back to bed. Leave Nellie alone.'

Jody felt a little afraid. He had never heard Billy speak like that before.

'I wanted to see Nellie,' Jody said. 'I can't sleep.'

Then Billy spoke again, but more softly.

'Well, you go to bed. Don't worry. I'll get you a good colt.'

Jody walked slowly out of the barn. He was not happy. At one time he had always believed Billy. But then Gabilan had died.

As Jody went through the kitchen, he knocked into a chair.

'Who's there? What's the matter?' Carl Tiflin called out.

'What's the matter, Carl?' Mrs Tiflin said sleepily.

Then Carl Tiflin came out of the bedroom with a candle.

'What are you doing?' he said to Jody.

'I went to see the mare,' said Jody.

'Listen,' Carl Tiflin said. 'Nobody knows more about colts than Billy. You can leave everything to him.'

'But Gabilan died,' Jody suddenly said.

'Don't you blame Billy for Gabilan's death,' Carl Tiflin said angrily. 'If Billy can't save a horse, nobody can!'

7

Billy Keeps His Promise

Jody went back to bed and closed his eyes. Suddenly Billy shook his shoulder.

'Get up and hurry,' Billy said.

Then Billy turned and walked out of the room.

'What's the matter?' Mrs Tiflin called. 'Is that you, Billy?'

'Yes, ma'am.'

'Is Nellie ready?' Mrs Tiflin asked.

'Yes, ma'am,' Billy replied.

'All right, I'll get up and heat some water,' said Jody's mother.

Jody dressed quickly and ran to the barn with Billy. In the barn, Nellie was standing very still. Then she suddenly bent down on her front legs. The mare's whole body moved. Then stopped. But in a few moments she started again.

'There's something wrong,' Billy said.

He felt the mare's stomach.

'Oh, God!' he said. 'Something's wrong.'

And Nellie started moving again. Billy pushed hard against her stomach. He pushed very hard and Nellie cried out with pain.

'It's wrong,' Billy said, 'the colt's the wrong way round.'

Billy carefully felt Nellie's stomach again. He looked at Jody for a long time. Then Billy stepped back and picked up a hammer.

'Go outside, Jody!' Billy said.

But Jody stood still and stared.

'Go outside, Jody!' Billy shouted again.

Jody did not move.

Billy walked up close to Nellie's side.

'Turn your face away, Jody!' he shouted. 'Turn your face away!'

Jody turned his face sideways. Billy talked very quietly to Nellie. Then Jody heard the sound of the hammer. Nellie let out a loud scream and the hammer rose and fell again. Nellie fell heavily on her side and shook for a moment.

Billy bent over the mare's big stomach. His knife was in his hand. Billy pushed the knife into Nellie's stomach and made a hole. Then Billy dropped the knife and pushed his arms in the hole. He pulled out a big, white bag. He tore a

51

'Turn your face away, Jody!' he shouted. 'Turn your face away!'

hole in the bag with his teeth. A little black head came out of the hole.

Jody saw two little wet ears and he heard the colt breathing. Billy held the colt in his arms and looked at it. Then Billy walked slowly over and laid the colt at Jody's feet.

Billy's face and arms were dripping with blood. His body was shaking, but he spoke softly.

'There's your colt,' he said. 'I promised, and there it is. I had to kill Nellie. I had to. Go and get some hot water. Wash the colt and dry him. You'll have to feed him yourself. But you've got your colt now. I promised you a colt.'

Jody looked at the wet, breathing colt. The little animal tried to raise its head. The colt's eyes were a dark blue.

'Will you go for the water now! Go now,' Billy shouted.

Then Jody turned and ran out of the barn. It was light outside. Jody tried to be happy. He had his own colt at last. But all he saw was Billy Buck's bloody face and tired eyes.

POINTS
FOR
UNDERSTANDING

Points for Understanding

THE GIFT

1

1 Who was Billy Buck?
2 How old was Jody?
3 Why did Mrs Tiflin ring the triangle?
4 Why were Carl Tiflin and Billy going to Salinas?
5 What two jobs did Jody do in the evening?

2

1 After supper, Jody sat by the fireplace. What did his father tell him to do?
2 What did Jody see in the stall the next morning?

3

1 Carl Tiflin told Jody to look after the pony. What three things did Jody have to do?
2 What name did Billy and Jody give the pony?
3 Why was Jody not able to take the pony to school with him?

4

1 Why did Jody not ride the pony?
2 Jody's friends wanted to take the pony out into the corral. Why did Jody say 'no'?
3 What had Jody forgotten to do?
4 Why was Jody's mother proud of her son?

5

1 Why did Jody always listen carefully to Billy Buck?
2 What happened to Gabilan when it rained for a whole week?

3 One day the sun came out brightly. What did Jody do?
4 Where were Carl Tiflin and Billy Buck going that day?
5 Jody was afraid it might rain. What did Billy say to him?

6

1 What had happened to Gabilan during the day?
2 Jody led Gabilan into the barn. What did he do next?
3 Jody's mother wasn't worried about Gabilan. Why not?
4 'Gabilan has got a little cold,' Billy told Jody. Did Jody believe Billy?

7

1 Why did Jody walk home slowly after school?
2 How did the steam help Gabilan?
3 Who filled the wood box on Friday evening?
4 What did Billy do to the lump in the pony's neck?
5 Who slept in the barn on Saturday night?
6 What happened to Gabilan during the night?

8

1 Why was Jody glad when Billy came into the barn?
2 Why did Billy cut a hole in the pony's neck?
3 Why was Billy angry with Carl Tiflin?

9

1 How did Jody know that Gabilan was dying?
2 Where was Gabilan when Jody woke up?
3 Why were the buzzards standing round the pony?
4 'The buzzard didn't kill the pony,' said Carl Tiflin to Jody. 'Don't you know that?' Why was Billy so angry at Carl's question?

THE GREAT MOUNTAINS

1

1 Did Jody learn very much about the mountains?
2 What was the old man's name?
3 What did the man say?

2

1 Where was the old man born?
2 Why had he come back?
3 Where was he going to sleep that night?
4 What did he have to do next morning?

3

1 Jody talked to the old man. What did he talk about?
2 Why did Carl Tiflin want to shoot old Easter? Did Jody believe him?
3 What was Gitano's secret?
4 At breakfast, Mrs Tiflin asked, 'Where's the old man?' What was Carl Tiflin's answer?

4

1 The old man had disappeared.
  (a) Where was he going?
  (b) How was he getting there?
  (c) What was he carrying?

THE PROMISE

1

1 Why was Mrs Tiflin angry with Jody?
2 Who was Nellie?
3 Where did Jess Taylor live?
4 Why was Jody going to visit Jess Taylor?

2

1 Billy Buck said, 'It's a long time to wait.' What did he mean?
2 What was Jody's reply to Billy?
3 'He'll kill her!' Jody cried.
   (a) Who is *he*?
   (b) Who is *her*?

3

1 Why did Billy feel Nellie's stomach?
2 Why was Jody worried when he talked to Billy about Nellie's colt?
3 Why was Billy Buck not so worried?

4

1 Nellie had changed. What was the difference?
2 Why did Carl want Jody to watch the birth of the colt?
3 Why did Billy feel proud of himself?
4 Jody also felt very proud. Why?

5

1 Why did Jody feel Nellie's stomach so often?
2 Jody asked Billy, 'Is Nellie all right?' Why did he ask this?
3 'Is Nellie going to be all right?' Jody asked again. What was Billy's reply?

6

1 At one time, Jody had always believed Billy. Something had changed this. What was it?

7

1 Why did Billy wake up Jody?
2 'There's something wrong,' Billy said. What was wrong?
3 Billy told Jody to turn his face away. Why?
4 Billy had promised Jody a colt. Did he keep his promise?
5 Why was Jody unhappy?

FICTION
The Pearl
The Wayward Bus
Cannery Row
The Moon is Down
The Grapes of Wrath
The Long Valley
The Red Pony
Of Mice and Men
Saint Katy the Virgin
In Dubious Battle
Tortilla Flat
To a God Unknown
The Pastures of Heaven
Cup of Gold
East of Eden
Sweet Thursday
The Short Reign of Pippin IV
The Winter of Our Discontent

GENERAL
A Russian Journal
Bombs Away
Sea of Cortez (*in collaboration with Edward F. Ricketts*)
The Forgotten Village (*documentary*)
The Log from the Sea of Cortez
Once There Was A War
Travels with Charley
America and Americans

PLAYS
The Moon is Down
Of Mice and Men
Burning Bright

Road to Nowhere *by John Milne*
The Black Cat *by John Milne*
Don't Tell Me What To Do *by Michael Hardcastle*
The Runaways *by Victor Canning*
The Red Pony *by John Steinbeck*
The Goalkeeper's Revenge and Other Stories *by Bill Naughton*
The Stranger *by Norman Whitney*
The Promise *by R.L. Scott-Buccleuch*
The Man With No Name *by Evelyn Davies and Peter Town*
The Cleverest Person in the World *by Norman Whitney*
Claws *by John Landon*
Z for Zachariah *by Robert C. O'Brien*
Tales of Horror *by Bram Stoker*
Frankenstein *by Mary Shelley*
Silver Blaze and Other Stories *by Sir Arthur Conan Doyle*
Tales of Ten Worlds *by Arthur C. Clarke*
The Boy Who Was Afraid *by Armstrong Sperry*
Room 13 and Other Ghost Stories *by M.R. James*
The Narrow Path *by Francis Selormey*
The Woman in Black *by Susan Hill*

For further information on the full selection of
Readers at all five levels in the series, please refer
to the Heinemann Guided Readers catalogue.

Heinemann English Language Teaching
A division of Reed Educational and Professional Publishing Limited
Halley Court, Jordan Hill, Oxford OX2 8EJ

OXFORD   MADRID   FLORENCE   ATHENS   PRAGUE
SÃO PAULO   MEXICO CITY   CHICAGO   PORTSMOUTH (NH)
TOKYO   SINGAPORE   KUALA LUMPUR   MELBOURNE
AUCKLAND   JOHANNESBURG   IBADAN   GABORONE

ISBN 0 435 27204 7

Illustrated by Peter Dennis
Typography by Adrian Hodgkins
Cover by Roger Jones and Threefold Design
Typeset in 11.5/14.5 pt Goudy
by Joshua Associates Ltd, Oxford
Printed and bound in Malta by Interprint Limited

96 97 10 9 8 7 6 5